For Detroit
With love,

THN

★

To the tenacious spirit of Detroit in all of us!

NT

©Susan Montgomery/Shutterstock

Text Copyright © 2019 Trinka Hakes Noble
Illustration Copyright © 2019 Nicole Tadgell
Design Copyright © 2019 Sleeping Bear Press

Sleeping Bear Press™

2395 South Huron Parkway, Suite 200, Ann Arbor, MI 48104
www.sleepingbearpress.com © Sleeping Bear Press

Printed and bound in the United States.
10 9 8 7 6 5 4 3 2 1

Library of Congress Cataloging-in-Publication Data
Names: Noble, Trinka Hakes, author. | Tadgell, Nicole, 1969- illustrator.
Title: A fist for Joe Louis and me / Trinka Hakes Noble ; Nicole Tadgell.
Description: Ann Arbor, MI : Sleeping Bear Press, [2019] | Series: Tales of
young Americans | Summary: In Depression-era Detroit, Gordy and Ira, one
African-American and one German-Jewish, bond over a shared interest in
boxing as America awaits the rematch between Joe Louis and Max Schmeling.
Identifiers: LCCN 2019003998 | ISBN 9781534110168 (hardcover)
Subjects: | CYAC: Friendship--Fiction. | Boxing--Fiction. | Family
life--Michigan--Detroit--Fiction. | African Americans--Fiction. |
Germans--Michigan--Fiction. | Jews--United States--Fiction. | Detroit
(Mich.)--History--20th century--Fiction.
Classification: LCC PZ7.N6715 Fis 2019 | DDC [E]--dc23
LC record available at https://lccn.loc.gov/2019003998

A FIST FOR JOE LOUIS AND ME

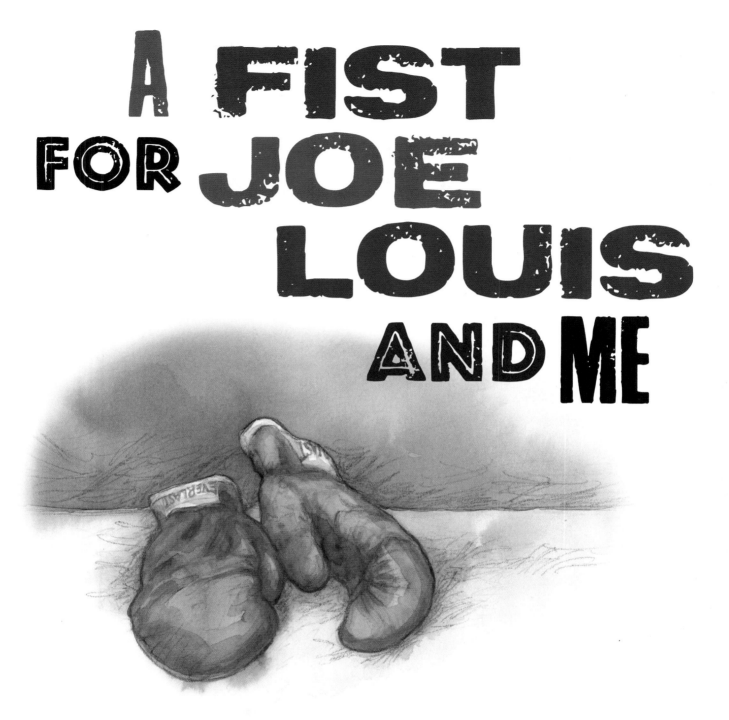

TRINKA HAKES NOBLE

AND ILLUSTRATED BY

NICOLE TADGELL

PUBLISHED by SLEEPING BEAR PRESS • TALES of YOUNG AMERICANS SERIES

Every Friday, after he came home from working at the auto plant, my father gave me a boxing lesson. "Keep your fists up, Gordy," he'd say, holding up his big strong hands like targets.

Then, after dinner, we'd listen to the Friday Night Fights on the radio. Everyone did in Detroit, especially when Joe Louis was boxing.

Detroit made two things: great boxers and cars, millions of cars. But when the Great Depression came, people stopped buying cars. Times got hard in Detroit. But we still had Joe Louis in our corner.

By 1937 there was talk of war with Nazi Germany. That fall my father lost his job, and his big strong hands turned into tense clenched fists.

So my mother started sewing for Mr. Rubinstein, a tailor. The Rubinsteins had fled from Nazi Germany so they would be safe.

"It's not much money," she said, "but it will keep us in groceries."

On Mondays, Mr. Rubinstein and his son, Ira, delivered pieces of sewing to my mother.

"Gordy, you and Ira go out and play. Mr. Rubinstein and I need to go over this work."

Ira was the new kid in my class. I'd never played with him, so I asked, "What do you want to play, Ira?"

Ira looked down and shuffled his feet. "Boxing," he answered shyly.

"Boxing?" I asked with surprise. "What do you know about boxing?"

Everyone in Detroit knew about boxing. But Ira hadn't been here long.

"Not much, but I listen to the Friday Night Fights with my father. Our favorite boxer is Joseph Louis."

Again I was surprised. We listened, too, at least we used to. After my father lost his job, he lost interest in boxing and the Friday Night Fights.

"First of all, Ira, it's Joe Louis, not Joseph Louis. Detroit is Joe Louis's hometown. He got his start here. Detroit is Joe Louis and Joe Louis is Detroit, okay? Now put up your dukes."

"Dukes? What are dukes?" asked Ira.

I almost said, "Oh, come on, everyone knows what dukes are," but I could tell by the serious look on Ira's face that he didn't know.

"Your fists, Ira. Put up your fists."

I was taller than Ira and my hands were big, like my father's. When I put up my fists, just to show Ira, he jumped back.

"Are you, ah, are you going to hit me?"

"Gosh, no, Ira! I've never hit anyone in my life!"

From then on, when Mr. Rubinstein delivered sewing, Ira and I would pretend to box out in the back alley behind the garage. I showed Ira how to bob and weave and protect his face.

Sometimes Ira got to be Joe Louis and sometimes I did. Then Ira would have to be Max Schmeling, the German, Joe's biggest opponent. We'd spar, bob and weave, then throw fake punches and act out pretend knockouts. We'd make sounds like the cheering crowds. We never really hit each other.

One day I said, "Ira, we need to make up some boxing names."

Ira grinned. "Okay, I'll be Iron Ira and you can be Gordy Steel."

"Yeah!" I laughed. "We're iron and steel, tough and strong, just like Detroit."

Ira laughed, too. Now it felt like Ira had always been a Detroit kid, like me.

Then, one day at school during recess, Nicky Benkowski started picking on Ira, calling him skinny and puny. Nicky was older and bigger than both of us. At first Ira ignored him, but Nicky wouldn't stop. He shoved Ira. Then it happened. Ira turned . . .

and put up his dukes!

Nicky laughed, but Ira didn't back down.

"No, Ira! Don't!" I shouted. "He'll flatten you!"

Just then a teacher came out on the playground, so Nicky backed down.

"Watch your back, you skinny little punk! We got unfinished business!"

I wondered then, *Has anyone ever yelled at Joe Louis like that? What would he do?*

That spring, Detroit was rainy and gloomy, which matched my father's face. When Mr. Rubinstein and Ira came, my father would disappear into the kitchen. It bothered him that he was still out of work and my mother was paying for more than groceries now.

One day Mr. Rubinstein followed him and started talking about boxing.

"How about that Yosef Louis, huh? And this rematch with the German Max Schmeling. They're saying the German is superior and Louis can't win. They're calling it the Fight of the Century. But it feels like a fight between America and Nazi Germany, no?"

My father looked surprised. "You know about this fight?"

"Plenty I know," Mr. Rubinstein said. "My people and your people, we have much in common, Mr. Williams. This fight is for us, too."

I didn't know what Mr. Rubinstein was talking about, but my father did.

"It's for all of us," he said as he stood and reached out his big hand. Mr. Rubinstein reached out his hand, too.

I wasn't sure why, but their handshake felt important, like reaching across something far greater than our kitchen table.

After that, we never missed the Friday Night Fights on the radio. They were building up to the big rematch between Joe Louis and Max Schmeling for the World Heavyweight Championship. It was so important they were holding it in Yankee Stadium on June 22. I couldn't wait!

But that day after school, Nicky Benkowski cornered Ira and me in the back alley. Immediately Ira put up his dukes.

I knew Joe Louis wouldn't let Ira go it alone. Sometimes you have to do the right thing, even if you don't want to. So I stepped in front of Ira and put up my dukes.

"Okay, Gordy, you wanna go first? I can whip both of you easy!"

Nicky was big and clumsy. He came at me like a bull and took a swing, but I bobbed. Nicky almost lost his balance.

It seemed I could hear Joe Louis's voice in my ear. *That's it, Gordy. Keep him off balance. Tire him out.*

I don't know how, but I began to dance around Nicky, bobbing and weaving.
Nicky whirled around, trying to hit me. But I kept it up, faster and faster.

By now Nicky was panting and throwing wild punches, his red face scowling at me.

But Joe's voice was calm. *Be patient, Gordy. Wait. Then take your best shot.*
You'll only get one, so make it count.

I didn't know if I had a best shot, but whatever I had, it would be for Ira and me.
So I took a deep breath and threw a punch. I must have caught Nicky off-balance,
because he went sprawling, facedown. Slowly he got to his knees, spitting out dirt.

"Lucky punch, kid," he sputtered, then stumbled off.

Ira held my fist up in the air. "Gordy Steel! The winner!"

But I didn't feel like a winner. I felt sick inside, and for a moment I wondered if Joe Louis ever did, too.

That night Mr. Rubinstein and Ira came to our house.

"Gordy, look who's here," my father said. "Please, come in.
We've got the radio tuned in to the big fight."

Ira and I stretched out on the floor with a big bowl of popcorn.

Over the radio, the ringside announcer was shouting above the roar
of the crowd. Then . . . ***CLANG*** . . . went the bell.

> *And Joe Louis is in the center of the ring,*
> *Max going around him. . . .*
> *Louis with the old one two.*
> *First a left and then the right. . . .*

We all jumped to our feet, popcorn spilling everywhere.

> *Louis fights desperately to bring up a*
> *left to the jaw and a right to the body. . . .*
>
> *Schmeling is down. . . .*
> *Five, six, seven, eight.*
> *The fight is over—on a technical knockout.*
> *Max Schmeling is beaten in one round!*

We burst into cheers!

"They don't call Joe the Brown Bomber
for nothing!" shouted my father.

Later Ira and I slipped outside to the back alley.
The streetlight had just come on, so we shadowboxed
against the garage wall. That night we both got to be
Joe Louis, the Brown Bomber . . . the champ!

When our fathers came outside, Mr. Rubinstein took Ira's hand. "Time to go home, son," he said. My father reached for my hand, too. Then he shook Mr. Rubinstein's hand goodbye. And for a moment the four of us stood there, hand in hand, quietly connected.

That night I felt as strong as Joe Louis.

The Fight of the Century had lasted only two minutes and four seconds, but I knew it would be with Ira and me for the rest of our lives.

AUTHOR'S NOTE

In the heart of Detroit, displayed in a plexiglass case in Cobo Center, sits an unassuming bronzed boxing glove. Underneath is a sign that reads: *THE GLOVE THAT FLOORED NAZI GERMANY . . . Through the generosity of Michigan Jewish Sports Hall of Fame, Fred and Marguerite Guinyard*

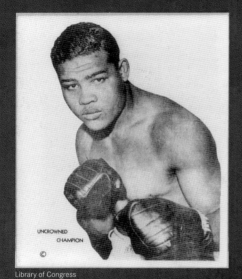

UNCROWNED
CHAMPION

Library of Congress

I first saw this boxing glove some years ago when I was attending a Michigan Reading Association conference. When I realized that it was the very same boxing glove that Joe Louis wore when he knocked out German boxer Max Schmeling in the Fight of the Century in 1938, I was floored! In fact, I couldn't move I was so captivated by Joe Louis's boxing glove. That fight stood for so much more than just the World Heavyweight Championship title. Millions of people around the world listened to the radio broadcast of that fight. When Joe Louis knocked out Max Schmeling in the very first round, it gave the world hope during the dark days of the Great Depression and the coming of World War II with Nazi Germany. I knew I had to write a story for young readers about the importance of this event.

Joseph Louis Barrow was born in rural Alabama, one of eight children. He moved to Detroit in 1926 when he was a boy of twelve, during the first Great Migration north. It must have been hard for him to adjust to a big city, but his mother was a stable and loving influence on Joe, and she taught him to always do the right thing. So I wove these two elements into my story: being a new kid in Detroit and doing the right thing.

From my Michigan childhood, I fondly remember trips to Detroit for family outings and school events, so I made the city a character in my story, too.

Joe Louis held the World Heavyweight Championship title longer than any other fighter, making him a boxing legend. Not only did he become a symbol for the city of Detroit, he was an American icon for the whole world. Later, Joe Louis and Max Schmeling became friends and remained close for the rest of their lives. Joe Louis was a true American hero.

—Trinka Hakes Noble

Max Schmeling and Joe Louis pose for photo during Max's 1954 tour of the U.S., Chicago, IL, 1954.